Dear Parents and Educators,

W9-AET-957

Welcome to Penguin Young Readers! As parents and educators, you know that each child develops at his or her own pace—in terms of speech, critical thinking, and, of course, reading. Penguin Young Readers recognizes this fact. As a result, each Penguin Young Readers book is assigned a traditional easy-to-read level (1–4) as well as a Guided Reading Level (A–P). Both of these systems will help you choose the right book for your child. Please refer to the back of each book for specific leveling information. Penguin Young Readers features esteemed authors and illustrators, stories about favorite characters, fascinating nonfiction, and more!

Fox on Stage

LEVEL **3**

GUIDED READING LEVEL **J**

This book is perfect for a **Transitional Reader** who:
• can read multisyllable and compound words;
• can read words with prefixes and suffixes;
• is able to identify story elements (beginning, middle, end, plot, setting, characters, problem, solution); and
• can understand different points of view.

Here are some **activities** you can do during and after reading this book:
• Idioms: An *idiom* is a word or group of words that has a special meaning when read all together. The author of this book uses several idioms. Reread the following idioms and discuss their meanings: "down in the dumps" (page 7), "pick up her spirits" (page 7), "set off" (page 14), "tore away" (page 15), and "face the music" (page 20).
• Situational Irony: Situational irony happens when the outcome of a situation is the opposite of what is expected. The author uses situational irony in his writing. Discuss why Grannie loves Fox's "dumb" movie and why the audience thought Fox's play was funny even though he thought it was a disaster.

Remember, sharing the love of reading with a child is the best gift you can give!

—Bonnie Bader, EdM
  Penguin Young Readers program

*Penguin Young Readers are leveled by independent reviewers applying the standards developed by Irene Fountas and Gay Su Pinnell in *Matching Books to Readers: Using Leveled Books in Guided Reading*, Heinemann, 1999.

For Anita Lobel—JM

Penguin Young Readers
Published by the Penguin Group
Penguin Group (USA) Inc., 375 Hudson Street, New York, New York 10014, USA
Penguin Group (Canada), 90 Eglinton Avenue East, Suite 700, Toronto, Ontario M4P 2Y3, Canada
(a division of Pearson Penguin Canada Inc.)
Penguin Books Ltd, 80 Strand, London WC2R 0RL, England
Penguin Ireland, 25 St Stephen's Green, Dublin 2, Ireland (a division of Penguin Books Ltd)
Penguin Group (Australia), 707 Collins Street, Melbourne, Victoria 3008, Australia
(a division of Pearson Australia Group Pty Ltd)
Penguin Books India Pvt Ltd, 11 Community Centre, Panchsheel Park, New Delhi—110 017, India
Penguin Group (NZ), 67 Apollo Drive, Rosedale, Auckland 0632, New Zealand
(a division of Pearson New Zealand Ltd)
Penguin Books, Rosebank Office Park, 181 Jan Smuts Avenue, Parktown North 2193, South Africa
Penguin China, B7 Jaiming Center, 27 East Third Ring Road North,
Chaoyang District, Beijing 100020, China

Penguin Books Ltd, Registered Offices: 80 Strand, London WC2R 0RL, England

Copyright © 1993 by James Marshall. All rights reserved. First published in 1993 by Dial Books for
Young Readers, an imprint of Penguin Group (USA) Inc. Published in a Puffin Easy-to-Read edition
in 1996. Published in 2013 by Penguin Young Readers, an imprint of Penguin Group (USA) Inc.,
345 Hudson Street, New York, New York 10014. Manufactured in China.

The Library of Congress has cataloged the Dial edition under
the following Control Number: 91046740

ISBN 978-0-14-038032-3   10 9 8 7 6 5 4 3

ALWAYS LEARNING   PEARSON

PENGUIN YOUNG READERS

LEVEL 3
TRANSITIONAL READER

FOX ON STAGE

by James Marshall

Penguin Young Readers
An Imprint of Penguin Group (USA) Inc.

FOX
ON FILM

When Grannie Fox had a bad spill

on the ski slopes,

she broke both legs.

"Grannie Fox will have to be

in the hospital for some time,"

said Doctor Ed.

"Old bones take longer to heal."

"Oh, what do *you* know?"

said Grannie.

But Doctor Ed was right.

Grannie had to stay in the hospital

for weeks and weeks.

"I'm so bored I could scream,"

she said.

"Grannie is down in the dumps,"
said Fox.
"We should do something to
pick up her spirits."
Then Fox got one of his great ideas.

"Louise and I are going to make a video for Grannie," said Fox.

"How sweet," said Mom.

"But if anything happens to my camera . . ."

"I know what I'm doing," said Fox.

The next day the video was finished.

Fox's friends came to watch.

"This better be good," said Carmen.

"I'm very busy."

Fox put in the tape.

"Here I am taking out the trash," said Fox.

"This is me in my new shoes," said Fox.

"Hm," said Dexter.

"Me, flossing my teeth," said Fox.

"*How* exciting," said Carmen.

"Me again," said Fox.

"So we see," said Dexter.

"Care to watch it again?" said Fox.

"Certainly not," said Carmen.

"You've wasted our time."

"What was wrong with it?"

said Fox.

"It was *dumb*," said Dexter.

"I liked it, Fox," said Louise.

The next day Fox tried again.

He put a new tape in the camera
and set off.

This time he left Louise at home.

"You're so mean," said Louise.

Just down the block Fox filmed

Mrs. O'Hara trying on her new corset.

"Smile!" said Fox.

"Monster!" cried Mrs. O'Hara.

And Fox tore away.

Down a dark alley

Fox filmed some bad dogs.

They were up to no good.

"Catch that fox!" they cried.

And Fox ran away.

In the park Fox saw Officer Tom

smooching with his girlfriend.

"Nice shot!" said Fox.

"You'll be sorry!" cried Officer Tom.

But Fox got away.

Fox went to the hospital

to show Grannie his new video.

But Grannie and Louise

were already watching one.

"This is Fox flossing his teeth,"

said Louise.

"Wow!" said Grannie.

"Don't watch that!" cried Fox.

"It's dumb!"

"What do you know?" said Grannie.

"We just *love* it."

At Fox's house some folks were waiting.

"That's him!" cried Mrs. O'Hara.

Maybe they don't like being
movie stars, thought Fox.
And he went inside to face the music.

FLYING FOX

Fox and the gang
went to a magic show.
"I hope this guy is good,"
said Dexter.
"It's probably just a lot
of dumb tricks with scarves,"
said Fox.
"Anybody can do it."
And they sat down in
the very first row.
The lights went down.
And the curtain went up.

Mr. Yee, the World's Greatest Magician,
came forward.

"Welcome to the show,"
he said.

"Some parts will be *very* scary!"

"Oh, sure," whispered Fox.

"Let the magic begin!"
cried Mr. Yee.

First Mr. Yee did a trick with scarves.

"I told you," said Fox.

Then Mr. Yee made his helper vanish.

"Ho-hum," said Fox.

Next Mr. Yee pulled a rabbit from a hat.

"Big deal," said Fox.

Next Mr. Yee put his helper to sleep.

"This is *so* dumb," said Fox.

"What's all the chatter?" said Mr. Yee.

"It's Fox!" called out Dexter.

"You don't say," said Mr. Yee.

"Come up onstage, Fox."

"You're going to get it!" said Dexter.

Fox went up onstage.

"Sit here, Mr. Smarty," said Mr. Yee.

"Let's see how brave you are."

"Brave?" said Fox.

"Abracadabra!" said Mr. Yee.

Slowly the chair rose in the air.

"Where are the wires?" said Fox.

"No wires," said Mr. Yee.

"Only magic."

Fox held on tight.

And the chair flew all over.

"I'd like to come down," said Fox.

"Oh my," said Mr. Yee.

"I forgot how to do this part."

"Try *Abracadabra*!" said Fox.

"Abracadabra," said Mr. Yee.

Fox came gently down.

And the show was over.

At home Fox told Louise to sit down.

"Abracadabra!" said Fox.

The chair did not move.

"Rats!" said Fox.

"You just need practice," said Mom.

FOX
ON STAGE

One Saturday morning
Fox and his friends
were just lying around.
"What a sad little group,"
said Mom.
"Why don't you *do* something?"
"The television is broken,"
said Fox.
"Oh, that *is* terrible!"
said Mom.
Then Fox had one of his
great ideas.

"Let's put on a play!" he said.

"We can charge everyone a dime."

"We'll get rich!" said Dexter.

"I'll buy a new car," said Carmen.

And they went to the library.

"Let's do a spooky play," said Carmen.

"We can scare all the little kids."

"Here's what you need,"
said Miss Pencil.

"It's called *Spooky Plays*.
My favorite is *The Mummy's Toe*."

"Oooh," said the gang.

Fox and the gang went home
to practice.

The Mummy's Toe was *very* scary.

Dexter played the mummy.

Carmen was the princess.

And Fox was the hero.

Soon things were moving right along.

Fox and Dexter worked hard

on the set.

And Carmen put up posters

all over town.

Mom and Louise helped out
with the costumes.

"Hold still," said Mom.

"I hope I'm scary enough,"
said Dexter.

It was time for the play.

Fox peeked out from
behind the curtain.
There was a big crowd.
"I hope everything goes okay,"
said Dexter.
"What could go wrong?" said Fox.

The curtain went up.

And the play began.

Right away Carmen forgot her lines.

"Well, I *did* know them,"

she said to the audience.

Then Dexter crashed through
the scenery.

"Whoops," said Dexter.

It was Fox's turn to appear.

Suddenly it began to rain.

Fox's beautiful paper costume

fell apart in front of everyone.

"What do we do now?" said Carmen.

"Pull the curtain down!"

Fox called out to Louise.

And Louise pulled with all her might.

The curtain came down.

"Who turned out the lights?"

cried Carmen.

"Where am I?" said Dexter.

"The play is ruined!" cried Fox.

"*Everything* went wrong!"

The next day

Fox heard some folks talking.

"That Fox really knows how
to put on a funny show," someone said.
"Funniest thing I ever saw,"
said someone else.

And Fox began to plan his next show.